Pizazz

VS THE DEMONS

IT'S NOT EASY
BEING SUPER…

Sophy Henn

SIMON & SCHUSTER

First published in Great Britain in 2022 by Simon & Schuster UK Ltd

1 3 5 7 9 10 8 6 4 2

Simon & Schuster UK Ltd
1st Floor, 222 Gray's Inn Road
London
WC1X 8HB

www.simonandschuster.co.uk
www.simonandschuster.com.au
www.simonandschuster.co.in

Simon & Schuster Australia, Sydney
Simon & Schuster India, New Delhi

A CIP catalogue record for this book is available from the British Library.

PB ISBN 978-1-3985-0580-3
eBook ISBN 978-1-3985-0581-0
eAudio ISBN 978-1-3985-0582-7

Printed and bound by CPI Group (UK) Ltd, Croydon, CR0 4YY

MIX
Paper from
responsible sources
FSC® C171272

MEET THE SUPERS ...
my mum
AKA ATOMIC
my dad
AKA ORE
my ANNOYING Little Sister
AKA RED
DRAGON
Wanda
1/2 dog 1/2 telephon

Grandma
AKA RAY
Gramps
AKA INFERNO
AUNTY BLAZE
SHE'S SO COOOOOOL
Uncle Teaser
Uncle Titano-ooooo
Jett
my super friend
Granny
my secret baddie friend
KAPOW
Aunty FURY
UH-OH

... AND THE NORMALS

Tom

Susie

my best friends from my old school

The bit where
I say hi . . .

Hi.
  My name is
PIZAZZ, and I am 9½

(for at least another month, I think)

and

I am

SUPER!

Yes, I do realise that sounds very **BIG-HEADED** and quite a bit **SHOW-OFFY** of me, but it really isn't.

I might occasionally be rather proud of my **AMAZING nail varnish collection** (85% **BLACK**, 15% very nearly **BLACK**), and I do like my hair (I mean, how could you not?), but the fact that I am **SUPER** really is NOT one of my favourite things about me. This is because when I say **SUPER** I don't mean **BRILL** or **FAB** or **GREAT**. What I mean is that . . .

...I am a

SUPERHERO.

Like this lot.

Except also NOT.

16

And, trust me, being **SUPER** REALLY isn't ANYTHING to **SHOW OFF** about — it's actually quite rubbish. Every time we defeat a **BADDIE**, another one pops up, and it's usually *just* as my *favourite* TV programme has started, or *just* as I've painted my nails, or *just* as I have washed my hair and need to dry it **properly** (not have it dry **naturally** while I *WHIZZ* about saving Earth, so it goes all fUNNy and then I can't do **A THING** with it).

And I definitely don't want to **SHOW OFF** my (not so) **SUPER POWER**. I actually want to do the exact opposite and never have to use it ever again. Especially not in public. What is my **SUPER POWER**? Well, imagine the most embarrassing thing **EVER** and then times it by 100 . . . THAT'S what it is.

Because while my *family* are all fairly normal **SUPERHEROES**, with normal **SUPERHERO**

costumes and normal **SUPERHERO** powers, for some BRILLIANT* reason I got the **weirdest SUPER POWER** EVER, the **strangest** name in the HISTORY of **SUPERHEROES**, and then there's my **costume**. I mean, LOOK!

It really doesn't seem FAIR and no matter what Mum says, I really don't think I am actually going to grow into my cape. **EVER**.

SUPER POWER:
Turns into molten metal
NORMAL

SUPER POWER:
Fire
NORMAL

SUPER POWER:
Jazz hands which create a glitter storm
NOT NORMAL

SUPER POWER:
Human Torch
NORMAL

* Really NOT brilliant

As my family are nearly all embarrassing **SUPER WEIRDOS**, sometimes it's actually a relief to go to school. I know, I can't believe I said that either, especially as my school is a NORMAL school full of NORMAL people . . .

Well, other than my silly sister, **RED DRAGON**, and another **SUPERHERO** called **JETT** – but because **JETT** is good at sport and only has a tiny capelet everyone thinks she's **SUPER** cool. So, of course, me and my too-long cape and silly **SUPER** name don't stand out at all.

EYE ROLL

But I do have the best friends EVER (well, I think so)!

There's **Ivy**, Molly and Ed, and together we are known as **THE ECO COUNCIL**, because we are, well, the school **ECO COUNCIL**, obviously.

Oh, and we are also **The Cheese Squares** –
that's the band we formed for the school
TALENT SHOW, and as we haven't officially
split up I guess we are still a band. At least,
I think that's how it works . . .

UNFORTUNATELY . . .

Just like in my **SUPERHERO** life, there are *goodies* and **BADDIES** in my normal life too. I guess **Serena** and **The Populars** are the sort-of **BADDIES** at school. I also guess this is because **Serena** seems to think every single thing I have done since I moved here is either **ANNOYING** or **stupid** or both, and she has never missed an opportunity to let me know this. I have slowly realised that other than completely disappearing there's not much I can do about the situation. So sorry, **Serena**!

But also NOT sorry.

Ha!

Serena
(annoyed)

THINGS I DO THAT ANNOY SERENA	THINGS I DO THAT DO NOT ANNOY SERENA
Exist	
BREATHE	
Walk	
TALK	
Be in her CLASS	
EAT	
Live on the AME PLANET as her	

2

The bit where things get interesting . . .

Everything about my day was
fairly normal . . .

STANDARD TUESDAY CHECKLIST

RED DRAGON, my
annoying sister, was being
SUPER annoying – **CHECK!**

I had spilled some lunch on my
cape – **CHECK!**

My HAIR was looking GREAT –
CHECK!

Serena had made a SNARKY
comment about something or
other – **CHECK!**

The Populars had found
Serena's snarky comment
HILARIOUS – **CHECK!**

Dad was making something
involving CHiLLi for tea – **CHECK!**

And I was just thinking how nice it was to have had a totally **UN-SUPER**, normal, average-to-OK day when **WANDA**, our pet dog/direct telephone line to **Mission Control**, trotted into the kitchen, flopped on to the floor, rolled over, sat up suddenly, scratched her ear, looked extremely bored and then told us we had to go on a **mission**. OF COURSE WE DID.

Actually, for once, I didn't mind too much as Mum had told me that I had to tidy my room in the next half-hour. SO I figured if this **mission** went on for more than half an hour I couldn't possibly tidy my room!

MWAHAHAHAHAHAHA*

*EVIL LAUGH. I learned this from one of my secret **BADDIE** friends, **Perfecto**. I actually have two **BADDIE** friends, which is a little bit tricky as technically I am a goodie, so I have to keep them secret, and seeing each other can be quite difficult. That's why sometimes they pretend to aim a giant laser at Earth or steal the national supply of strawberry liquorice laces so **Mission Control** send me out to defeat them, and then instead of actual battling, we have a nice catch-up! Anyway, I like **evil laughing** a LOT, and I am quite a bit cross there is no *goodie* version . . . **Wholesome** chuckle? **Helpful** yelp? **Righteous** giggle?

3

The bit where it gets weird . . .

. . . and a bit itchy

While it was sort of nice (and **EXTREMELY surprising**) to know that someone had actually wanted to copy **ME**, I would have thought they would rather copy my ability to **paint my nails** with my eyes CLOSED (almost), my **guitar-legend** status (nearly), or being able to *SPEED ROLLER SKATE* **backwards** (but ONLY **clockwise** and, no, I don't know why either!). But why on earth would they want to copy my *NOT-SO-SUPER SUPER POWER*?

If I could copy ANY *SUPER POWER* I am pretty sure it wouldn't be jazz hands/glitter storm. Yes, that IS my *SUPER POWER*.

I know . . . pretty, erm, 'unique', isn't it?

Other than Samantha Mulligan having a nose bleed in English and **Serena** calling me **POOZAZZ** at morning break (I mean, funny if you're about five, but COME on?), everything about my Wednesday was pretty normal. But after yesterday's **SHOCK ENDING** I found myself on alert for something ***UNUSUAL*** to happen. And of course it did, because . . .

MY LIFE!

I had just got my lunch and was sitting at our usual table (the one nearish the window, with 'Fish and cheese sauce is WRONG' scratched into it) when Ed marched in. So far so normal, but then surprisingly he looked surprised to see me and asked how I had managed to get to the canteen before him AND get lunch?

Erm, by wandering down the corridor, joining the lunch queue and sitting down. **EYE ROLL**

And while the **EYE ROLL** wasn't strictly necessary, I still didn't expect Ed to react the way he did . . .

. . . which was to right back at me and say, '**Yeah, yeah, very clever**' and then point out that my mood had changed double fast as it was only five minutes ago that I was ruining his future as an international **rock star**.

Hmmmm? Er? WHAT?!? I was almost positive this hadn't actually happened (I can never be 100% sure because, you know, the **LLAMA** incident ***SHUDDER***) and told Ed this. But he was adamant and quite a bit cross with me for demanding that **MISS CASS** let me play the **maracas**. Apparently I thought I would be an even better **maracas** player than him, and it was probably MY THING and NOT his.

Well, Ed had a point as this didn't sound very nice at all, and even though I wasn't sure if I had actually done this or not, I was beginning to feel a bit **BAD** about it when . . .

Molly marched in, and as soon as she saw me her chin hit the floor and her eyebrows hit the ceiling. Well, not quite, but she did look **VERY surprised** and then she looked quite CROSS and then she said that I had a cheek.

I laughed and said I ACTUALLY had **two**, but Molly didn't laugh back.

In fact, this just seemed to make her **CROSSER** and she said she was glad I was happy – obviously **RUINING** her project had been super fun for me.

Hmmmmmm?

Er?

What NOW?

Molly sort of **SHOUT**/SPOKE at me about how by refusing to lend her my gel pens 'because I really cannot be even slightly bothered to go and get them', her project was now all sorts of BORING and a bit ruined.

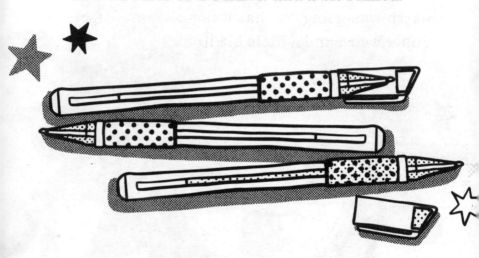

I said that of course she could borrow my gel pens (except for the gold one as it had already run out) and was just about to go and get them, but she said there was no point now as she had been *FORCED* to use felt tips, and while they were colourful, it just wasn't the same.

I didn't like this one bit. I mean, obviously having two of my best friends cross with me for things I was almost certain (curse you, **LLAMA**) I hadn't actually done was HORRIBLE. But it was the not-really-knowing-what-on-earth-was-going-on that was making me feel super weird and a little bit itchy.

MWAHA HAHAHA HAHA

BUT THEN . . .

Just when I thought things really couldn't get any weirder . . . guess what?

THEY DID.

Ivy came *zooming* into the canteen and she looked LIVID, which is very unusual, but as soon as she saw me she suddenly looked super surprised too, just like Molly and Ed. So I said, 'Don't tell me . . . I have just been really jealous or lazy and done something MEAN and HORRIBLE?'

And then Ivy got cross (well, cross for Ivy), and said that maybe it was a joke to me, but letting her down with the SAVE THE SQUIRRELS march she was organising wasn't funny to her. According to Ivy, I couldn't go because I was worried about maybe twisting my ankle while marching, or getting UV damage from the sun's rays, or possibly catching a really bad cold if it rained, and what if the squirrels didn't ACTUALLY want us to march and started dropping NUTS on our heads?

Hmmmmmm?

Er?

What now, WHAT?
While I could see the
thinking behind all of these
worries, I had to agree with
Ivy that it did seem a bit
unnecessarily PANICKY.

FURY!

Ivy just *eyerolled* and said
that if I really didn't want to go I should just
say so, not make up loads of nonsense to back
out of going.

Well, this time I knew it wasn't the **LLAMA**.
I wouldn't do that, to Ivy or the SQUIRRELS, and
I told Ivy so, but she said that was
ridiculous because **I JUST HAD.**

I started to feel weirder and itchier than EVER before. I knew my friends wouldn't make this up, and I didn't like them being **ANNOYED** with me at all. I was desperately trying to work out how I could have done all those things without even knowing, or even just ONE of those things, and I really, really couldn't and I thought I might be about to **POP** with the impossibleness of it all when we heard **SHOUTING**. It was a familiar **SHOUTING** voice, and I was VERY used to this **SHOUTING** voice because . . .

. . . it belonged to

ME.

And even though they were still **FUMING**,
I managed to convince Ivy, Molly and Ed (who
I had slightly calmed down by giving him my
pudding – a giant cookie, natch) to come with
me and see what was going on. We all
RACED down the corridor and followed the
SHOUTING to our form room and peeked
around the door.

*GASP*And there I was.

And I looked **livid**. Like, **REALLY livid**. And of all the people I could be **livid** at I had picked Serena. NOOOOOOOOO!

I tugged at Ivy's sleeve and asked her if I was really there, next to her, and not in our tutor room **SHOUTING** at Serena, and she said I definitely was. So how was it possible to have **two PIZAZZES** at once? A time loop? A really good **PIZAZZ impersonator**? A giant **PIZAZZ puppet**? A team of tiny dogs, standing on each other's shoulders wearing one of my spare costumes?

Ivy, Molly, Ed and I watched as the other me marched around Serena getting all cross about this and that and **SHOUTING** about one thing or another and even getting stroppy about her slouchy socks. (I would NEVER do that. Despite everything, I LOVE Serena's slouchy socks.)

Serena looked bored and disgusted

as usual, but also a bit UPSET, and even though she has never stopped to think about how UPSET she might make me, being the BIGGER person I did actually feel a bit bad. Then I remembered it wasn't *ME* me **SHOUTING** at Serena, and then I couldn't work out whether to feel **BAD** or not.

UGH, it was just my luck. Even the other me couldn't get things right with Serena, and how would I EVER live down **FURIOUS** other-me's *BAD* shenanigans? Serena would have it in for me FOR EVER. I was getting quite distracted and extremely confused by ALL of these thoughts, but then in the middle of EVERYTHING I realised I HAD to find out exactly what was going on and work out how to get back to just the one me . . .

. . . and I knew exactly where to **start** . . .

OH, GREAT.

So not only do I have to fight
ACTUAL *BADDIES* . . . now I
also get to fight *myself*.

The bit where it gets even weirder . . .

. . . but less itchy

LATER THAT DAY . . .

When I finally got home after school, I was a bit muddled about what to do. I mean, I wanted to tell everyone about all the other evilish me's, but **Mum** and **Dad** would probably just blame me for having so many not-very-nice me's inside myself in the first place. EYE ROLL So I just went to my room to do my homework.

But then I discovered it's really hard to concentrate on your homework when you have a Super Power Duplicator™ sitting in your room with lots and lots of lovely shiny buttons on it practically screaming to be pressed . . .

ZAPPPP! POW! ZIIIIING!!!!!!

. . . All I did was accidentally blast it a few times and instantly **Mum** was at the door, all: 'What on earth are you **firing** in your bedroom, PIZAZZ? We agreed **NO blasters**/

LASERS/bombs in the house! Show me what you are zapping **THIS INSTANT!!!**' 〔EYE ROLL〕

Then I realised there was no point in trying to hide it from **Mum** as she would probably find out anyway. Besides, I hadn't even slightly worked out what to do and she *MIGHT* actually be helpful . . . So I told **Mum** everything that had happened with **CopyCat** and the other slightly **Naughty Me**'s. Then I handed over the **Super Power Duplicator**™, which was quite a relief, and **Mum** had a few questions . . .

'So now there are **five** PIZAZZES?'

'Yes.'

'You are absolutely *certain* there are now **five** whole PIZAZZES?'

'Well, that's if you DON'T count the **original** me.'

'SO THERE ARE **SIX**?'

'M^mm_hm^mm.'

And then her face went a funny colour and she *RAN* to the kitchen to find **WANDA** so she could send a message to **Mission Control**.

Mum *ZOOMED OFF* with the Super Power Duplicator™, and I saw this as the perfect opportunity to raid the snack cupboard. I had just moved the chair to the cupboard, climbed up and was deciding between crisps and biscuits when she was BACK in the kitchen with ~~Aunty Blaze~~. Curse my indecision and their *SUPER SPEED!*

UGH.

Mum and ~~Aunty Blaze~~ sat me down and explained that, as much as they *wanted* to, they couldn't really HELP **me** with the other **BAD** ME's, or **THE DEMONS** as they were now known at **Mission Control**. Er, excuse me? **THE DEMONS**??? I mean, come on, that felt a bit much. I know I can get a smidge grumpy sometimes, and occasionally sarcastic, but **DEMONS**?!? *Really?*

2+2= PIZAZZ
HAS TO DEFEAT
ALL HER DEMONS

They explained that after someone **SUPER SMART** had done a few simple **CALCULATIONS** at **Mission Control** they had concluded I had to defeat **THE DEMONS** myself or it just wouldn't work, because they were part of me and only I could get rid of them.

WHAT? ON. MY. OWN. AGAIN?

I had only just defeated **Perfecto** on my own and now I had to beat **FIVE *DEMON* ME's**?!? I reminded **Mum** that only two minutes ago I was being **told off** for having a **blaster** in my room and now I was being sent out SOLO to defeat *The Five Awesome But Slightly BAD Me*'s (er, much better than '***THE DEMONS***', surely?). This all seemed ridiculously unfair and I am pretty sure I explained this in a sensible and mature way to **Mum** and **Aunty Blaze** . . .

WHIIIIIIINE

Once I had stopped *explaining* how unfair everything was, I told Mum and Aunty Blaze what CopyCat had said about these DEMONS also being FIVE more chances for her to copy my SUPER POWER. Did that mean I had to defeat THE DEMONS and stop CopyCat copying me AND do my maths homework? Then Mum and Aunty Blaze both put their heads to one side (always a worrying sign) and looked a bit sad, which I took as a YES.

UGH. **This was rubbish!** What was the point of living in a WHOLE *family* of **SUPERHEROES** if you had to do ALL the **SUPERING** yourself? Then I realised that I probably wasn't EVER going to get a better opportunity to get away with UNLIMITED **snacks** so I just looked a bit sad while I walked over to the cupboard and took as much as I could carry.

And **Mum** didn't say **anything**.

UH-OH.

Things must be BAD.

REALLY
BAD.

It was a good job I got as many **snacks** as I did, because when I got back to my room and looked for my pet guinea pig and soulmate, BERNARD, I found her on TOP of my bookshelf. I also found her **ON** my bed, **UNDER** my bed, in my school bag . . . and using my gym shorts as a trampoline . . .

FIVE BERNARDS?
HOW?

O°o°o°oooh, had I *accidentally* z^apped her when I was *accidentally* **blasting** the Super Power Duplicator™?

Erm, yes?

Oops.

My shock turned into excitement, but then it turned into **CONFUSION** . . . Which BERNARD was which? I lined them all up, trying to work out WHO was WHO.

After quite a bit of rearranging I'd cracked it! There was **ORIGINAL** BERNARD, *FABULOUS* BERNARD, *FABULOUSER* BERNARD, *FABULOUSEST* BERNARD and STINK-EYE. Then I realised it was getting late and there was homework to do (er, where were *THE DEMONS* now? The **FIVE OTHER ME**'s would actually be REALLY useful here . . . I wondered if any of them were good at maths) and then I wondered what my *DEMONS* would **actually** be. I mean, I know no one is **perfect**,

ORIGINAL BERNARD   FABULOUS BERNARD

or even **Perfecto**, but **FIVE**?! I started to try to make a mental list of possible **DEMONS**, but then got *sidetracked* by how completely UNFAIR it was that, whatever they were, my *actual* **DEMONS** had jumped out of my *actual* body, and now I had to battle them. I mean, really? It seemed QUITE A **LOT**. But all that wondering didn't help my maths homework one bit, so I **stopped**, finished the last sum and went to bed.

FABULOUSER BERNARD | FABULOUSEST BERNARD | STINK-EYE

I was having the MOST HORRIBLE, HORRIBLE dream, and in it there were FIVE MORE REDS – BLEURGH.

STINKY STINK BREATH

Each one was more IRRITATING and perky and *organised* and *smiley* than the other . . . SHUDDER! It was so completely **PETRIFYING** that I was actually quite relieved to be woken up by **WANDA** in her usual *kind* and considerate way.*

* By 'kind' I mean *STINKY* and by 'considerate' I mean SCRATCHY.

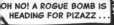

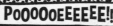

AND THEN . . .

Stupid stinky stink juice from **DABOMB**'s stupid stinky **STINK BOMB**. **UGH**.

As I stomped into the classroom, still slightly stinky, I suddenly remembered that one of my **DEMONS** had paid a visit to *Serena* the day before AND had been a bit **SHOUTY**. OH NO, surely this meant she was bound to be EXTRA *Serena*-ry to me today. Then I wondered if today could get **ANY WORSE?**

Er, yes. Yes, it could. Obviously . . . EYE ROLL

Firstly, even though I *deliberately* stared at the floor while *Sarah Wotton*'s arm was stretched up so high in the air it was practically in another atmosphere AND she was *waggling* her hand about like it was on fire AND her face was SO keen it looked like her head might blow up, *Mrs Harris* picked ME to read out a thing in the special **HAPPINESS ASSEMBLY** next week. Great.* EYE ROLL

* NOT great. The **opposite** of great. Un-great.

Mrs Harris said it should be fine as I had plenty of time to prepare.

Erm, I think I'll be the judge of that, Mrs Harris, and actually it might be a bit of a squeeze, what with having to BATTLE my **FIVE DEMONS**!

But she didn't look like she would change her mind and so instead I nodded my head, DIDN'T listen to the possibly **important** thing she was telling me, and slipped the piece of paper she gave me straight into my folder. It would keep. I mean, I had bigger things to **worry** about right now . . . EYE ROLL

The rest of the morning carried on in the SAME sort of way . . .

CHOCOLATE FACE ALL MORNING

CAPE CAUGHT

'LUCKY' BIRD POO

And that wasn't **even** the WHOLE DAY – it was just HALF the day. **UGH**. WHY was I the one that *CopyCat* had picked on? WHY did I have to have **FIVE** whole **annoying** *DEMONS* to defeat? WHY had the canteen run out of EVERYTHING except macaroni cheese (BLEURGH. It's just TOO cheesy)? And WHY did all of this have to happen to MEEEEEEE?

Even though I said all of this **very** LOUDLY, no one seemed to have any answers. Typical.

I could feel myself getting *crosser* and **CROSSER**, and I was almost certain that it wasn't going to help with any of the things I was actually *cross* about, but I didn't seem to want to stop . . .

ARRRRRRGHHHHHHH!

And then it happened . . .

LAWKS! IT'S AN ANGRY-OFF. THE PIZAZZES PICK FIGHTS ABOUT...

SCHOOL DINNERS...

GEL PENS...

GGRRRRR!!!

URRRRGH!!!

THE BEST NAIL VARNISH COLOURS...

AND ABOUT WHO IS THE BEST PIZAZZ...

5

The bit where Ed has a good idea . . .

As I stood in the playground looking up at giant **ANGRY DEMON ME**, I was finding it REALLY hard to think of a *plan* AND be **ANGRY** at the same time. So I decided to just be **ANGRY** . . . How dare I do this to ME, AT **SCHOOL** . . . IN FRONT OF **EVERYONE** . . . AND *Serena?*

SUPER EYE ROLL

I just couldn't bear it . . . but then I heard the sweet, soft sound of maracas getting closer and felt a tap on my shoulder. OBVIOUSLY it was Ed. And while no one could argue that the sound of them wasn't ever so soothing, with **ANGRY DEMON ME** STOMPING about all over the place AND *CopyCat* threatening to turn up at any moment I really DIDN'T HAVE TIME FOR MARACAS RIGHT NOW . . .

I *politely* (ish) told Ed this, and he said that I needed to chill, which is of course what every **ANGRY** person wants to hear!* Then he shook his maracas at me, fixed me with

a **goggly** stare and said that it was super obvious that ***ANGRY DEMON PIZAZZ*** was only getting BIGGER and BIGGER because I was getting ***ANGRIER*** and ***ANGRIER***.

PFFFFFT? I don't think so . . . But then Ed demonstrated this by telling me my hair was RUBBISH, which of course made me **cross** because it is **AWESOME** and I had had just about enough of everyone not realising that.

Right at that moment ***ANGRY DEMON PIZAZZ*** grew at least another metre, but then Ed quickly said that he was being silly and actually I had the COOLEST hair he had EVER seen.

That was more like it! And *amazingly*, ***ANGRY DEMON PIZAZZ*** actually shrank a tiny bit. Hmmmmm, maybe Ed was on to something and a something that sort of made sense of the whole '**me having to DEFEAT the *DEMON ME*'s on my own**' business.

---

*It is NOT. It is an actual fact that this only makes the person **crosser**. Now, please ONLY use this knowledge for **good** . . .
MWAHAHAHAHA!

Sometimes when you are *ANGRY* you can't NOT be *ANGRY* just like that, and although I knew my success DEPENDED on it I was struggling to

CALM DOWN!

So Ivy, Molly and Ed ran off and brought back as many pictures of HAMSTERS in HATS as they could find. It really helped.

Once those **SUPER CUTE fluff-balls** in their TEENY, TINY HATS had calmed me right down (I mean, how can you be *ANGRY* with ALL THAT CUTENESS?)

it

was

time . . .

RES

6

The bit where I get a bit worried . . .

wooooooo!
HOOOOOOOooo!
and

I had defeated **myself** and *surprisingly* that felt super **BRiLLIANT!** The rest of school was per-ritty good. I aced my spellings, almost completely avoided the ball during PE and didn't trip over my cape once . . . WINNING!

Ivy and I walked home together and talked about the other **DEMONS** and we agreed I should battle them all in the same way I had battled **ANGRY DEMON ME**, by keeping my cool and holding my nerve and not letting comments about my hair even *slightly* get to me. How hard could that be? I had totally got this. GO ME! But, like, **NORMAL me**, NOT **DEMON ME** . . .

obvs.

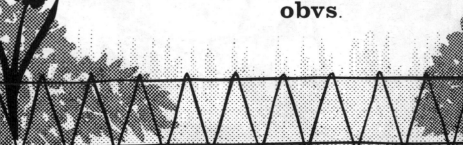

As I was t**ri**p**pi**ng over **WANDA** (I am CERTAIN she does it deliberately) I realised my **luck** had run out (that didn't last long) . . .
Yup, we had a **mission** to go on, but at least this one WASN'T against a *DEMON ME*!

As soon as I finished dinner, I ran to talk to the BERNARDS. This whole *DEMON* business was really worrying, especially as everyone was telling me I would be able to **DEFEAT** them on my own, but I hadn't even managed that when the first *DEMON* had showed up. If it hadn't been for Ed and hamsters in their hats it would have been a DISASTER. Probably. I did not have this sussed. Not even slightly, but knew the BERNARDS would reassure me and maybe even have some good *DEMON-BEATING* ideas . . .

Or maybe NOT. It turned out the BERNARDS were far too **busy** being *FABULOUS* and appeared to be forming some sort of girl band.

STINK-EYE

Well, all except STINK-EYE, who was extremely focused on giving EXCEPTIONAL STINK-EYE, which I guess is the point of her, really.

So I left them to it and *eventually* I worried myself to sleep . . .

My morning went brilliantly.*

7.30 a.m. – Roll out of bed, hit floor, WAKE UP.

7.45 a.m. – Wash face with SHAMPOO.

7.55 a.m. – Put shoes on WRONG feet.

8.00 a.m. – Realise I have forgotten to put socks ON. Take shoes OFF, put socks ON, put shoes on WRONG feet. **AGAIN**.

8.02 a.m. – Realise I haven't learned my times tables for MATHS.

8.03 a.m. – PANIC a bit.

8.05 a.m. – PANIC **SO MUCH** I get burps.

8.08 a.m. – Burp so much JUICE comes out of my **nose**.

8.10 a.m. – Trip over my CAPE as I leave for school.

*Not at all brilliantly.

By the time I arrived at school and met Ivy in the playground, I was already feeling a slight sense of **DOOM**. I was really, really, REALLY worried about when the other **DEMONS** were going to make an appearance and how I was going to defeat them. I got so worried that I started BURPING again and then I couldn't **STOP**, and then I started to worry that **Serena** might hear me and then I *agreed* with **me** that that would be AWFUL . . .

WAIT,

WHAT?

. . . Er, I mean, of course I *agreed* with me. **I** *AM* **ME** – I *agree* with everything I think. Well, ALMOST everything . . . but I don't usually hear **me** *agreeing* with **ME**, unless I said it myself, which I am *practically* positive I didn't.

AS ANXIOUS DEMON PIZAZZ WHISPERS WORRIES TO PIZAZZ...

... THIS WHIPS PIZAZZ UP INTO A FRENZY OF FRETFULNESS ...

... WHICH SWIRLS INTO A GIA VORTEX OF WORRY! OH NO!

HEY, PIZAZZ! WHICH DEMON YOU DO YOU THINK IT IS?

I DON'T KNOW!
AND I *CAN* BARELY EVEN *THINK* ABOUT IT! WAS THAT GIRL OVER THERE LOOKING AT ME FUNNY? I MEAN, I *KNOW* I AM SWIRLING ABOUT WITH A DEMON ME, BUT *STILL?* AND IT'S P.E. NEXT, ISN'T IT? I THINK I'M GOING TO BE *LATE*, BUT IF I AM *LATE* THEN I WILL GET INTO *BIG TROUBLE* AND THEN MUM WILL BE *FURIOUS* AND ...

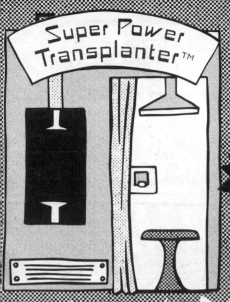

7

The bit where I get a bit jealous . . .

What a day! It was only 8.45 a.m. and I had already **defeated** the SECOND *DEMON ME*. It's no wonder I need to eat as many snacks as I do, what with everything I have to fit in.

I felt really **BAD** as *Ivy* and I got into medium-sized **trouble**, because after all the battling we were a bit late for register. Fortunately *Sarah Wotton* hadn't left to take the register to the

office yet (she is register monitor because OF COURSE SHE IS), so **Mrs Harris** marked us in and then reminded me about the **HAPPINESS ASSEMBLY**, checking I was all prepared . . . Erm, NO! I am in the middle of **defeating** my very own **DEMONS**, **Mrs Harris**, and not feeling exactly **happy** about it actually. But obviously I didn't really say that. I just said 'nearly' and **Mrs Harris** looked like she wasn't *sure* she believed me, but we left it there.

When I FINALLY sat down, Ivy was telling Molly and Ed all about the BATTLE with **ANXIOUS ME**. And, while I know she was pretty *helpful*, it seemed to me she was making it sound like she'd done almost EVERYTHING and I did pretty much nothing.

Er, excuse me, Ivy, but when I was *whirling* around 100 metres up in the air in a **vortex** of **worry** I didn't see you up there with me!

Yes, your ideas DID help, but let's just remember who the *ACTUAL* **SUPERHERO** is here. But then I felt **BAD** again because Ivy's ideas had possibly* saved the day.

Then I felt a bit **less BAD** when Molly and Ed kept *congratulating* her because I do actually do that practically

ALL THE TIME.

* Almost certainly

The rest of my morning wasn't much better . . .

Ed got picked to be **CAPTAIN** of the rounders team in PE and I didn't, which hardly seemed fair – he doesn't even LIKE **sport**!* (Neither do I, really, but I am almost positive I like sport a **bit** more than him . . . Maybe only a teeny **bit** . . . but that still counts, right?)

Claire Harding was REALLY showing off her new **PENCIL CASE** all the way through English. It was all patterny and sparkly, just like the one I really, REALLY wanted . . .

UGH!

And Brian Appleyard did NOT stop talking about his birthday trip to **PlasticbrickLand**, where I have NEVER been, not even to fight **BADDIES**, plastic or not . . .

It really felt like today was NOT **MY** day. Or indeed ANY day, in fact.

Where was *my* good stuff, hmmmm?

Why wasn't *I* team captain?

Where was *my* super cool **PENCiL CASE**?

WHY hadn't *I* been to **PlasticbrickLand**?

WHERE WAS *MY* GOOD STUFF?

Why didn't I have the good stuff?

WHHHHHHHY?

It really didn't seem fair . . .

Not. At. All.

* Unless you count playing the maracas as a **sport**, in which case he LOVES IT!

Then when Molly got the last sprinkly **doughnut** at lunchtime, well, that was IT . . . I just could NOT bear it. **IT WASN'T FAIR**. Any of IT. And Molly likes jelly and ice cream best – she isn't even really that **bothered** about **doughnuts**, not like I am anyway. Then my brain and mouth sort of **DISCONNECTED** and LOTS of words were spilling out of my mouth and I was fairly certain they WEREN'T very **NICE** ones because everyone was looking at me like I had grown a lizard's tail (just like Lizard Girl. I know, they REALLY didn't try hard with her name, right?).

Then, when I ran out of all the *not-so-nice* words, I stuck one of my fish fingers into Molly's **doughnut** (sort of like a breadcrumb-coated birthday candle) and I wished *me* a **'HAPPY EVERYONE ELSE EXCEPT PIZAZZ DAY!'** very LOUDLY.

Hang on, that could only mean one thing . . . Another of the **DEMONS** had arrived . . .

POOF JEALOUS DEMON PIZAZZ.

But the thing is, she had a point . . .
quite a FEW points, in actual fact . . .

GIVE ME MORE!

HEEEEAVE

THERE'S ALWAYS MORE, PIZAZZ!

UH-OH...

MWAHAHAHA!! NOW I'VE GOT YOU... YOU CAN'T EVEN MOVE! TOO EASY...

THERE'S NO QUICK GETAWAY FOR PIZAZZ...

WAHAHAHA!!

GIVE ME SUPER POWER DUPLICATOR V4 ™...

BUT OUR HERO IS DISAPPEARING UNDER ALL THE STUFF.

OH NO!

WAIT! I HAVE N IDEA...PIZAZZ, YOU VE TO GIVE SOMETHING AWAY.

OMETHING IMPORTANT... GIVE ME YOUR BOBBLES, PIZAZZ.

NO!! MINE!!!

I WANT MORE!!!

OH NO! THE GANG GIVE UP AND WALK AWAY...

SORRY, PIZAZZ

OH.

PIZAZZ (*PIZAZZ* PIZAZZ - OBVS) STARTS TO GIVE EVERYTHING BACK, PLUS A FEW EXTRAS

If no other single good thing came out of the **EPIC** battle against my very own *DEMON*, knowing that EVEN *Serena* couldn't help but *slightly* like my hair had made it ALL worthwhile!

Well, THAT and realising it's WAY *nicer* to **share** the GOOD stuff (stuff-stuff and words stuff) with everyone, rather than have it all to yourself – on your own.

The bit where I . . .

YAWN . . . Zzzz

THE NEXT DAY . . .

I was SUPER glad it was the weekend, so I decided to *celebrate* by seeing how long I could get away with staying in bed. As I lay there I could hear most of the BERNARDS working on their harmonies, and I wondered why all my *ME*'s couldn't be more like BERNARDS. But then I figured we can't all be just *FABULOUS*, *FABULOUSER* and *FABULOUSEST* (or even STINK-EYED), I suppose. Then I started to wonder what my **NEXT *DEMON*** would be – surely they couldn't be any **worse** than the ones I had already had?

Then I heard the door open and tried to stay really still, hoping that WHOEVER it was would think I was STILL *asleep* and just go away. But then whoever it was started **licking** my feet and I jumped up because it tickled too much, and WHO **LICKS** SOMEONE'S FEET TO **WAKE THEM UP** ANYWAY?

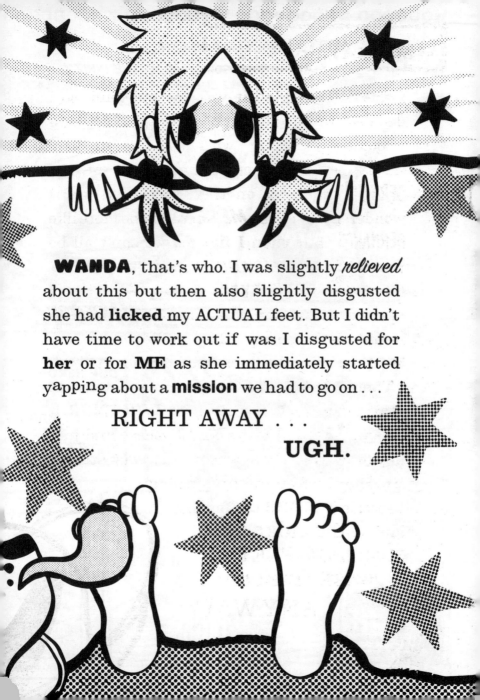

WANDA, that's who. I was slightly *relieved* about this but then also slightly disgusted she had **licked** my ACTUAL feet. But I didn't have time to work out if was I disgusted for **her** or for **ME** as she immediately started yapping about a **mission** we had to go on . . .

RIGHT AWAY . . .

UGH.

WELL, WHADDAYA KNOW . . .

SUPER SPEEDY, SUPER BADDIE *THE WHIZZ* IS, WELL, WHIZZING ABOUT ALL OVER THE PLACE AND GETTING UP TO ALL SORTS OF TROUBLE. IT'S UP TO YOU LOT TO STOP HIM . . . BUT HOW?!

WHAT? NO, I DON'T KNOW, YOU'RE THE SUPERHEROES . . .

REALLY!

CATCH ME IF YOU CAN . . . HA-HA!

WHIZZZZ

YAWN

OUR HEROES *ZOOM OFF* TO TRY TO STOP T SPEEDY BADDIE, BUT IT SEEMS PIZAZZ IS NOT EXACTLY 'ON IT'

WHEN THEY ARRIVE **THE WHIZZ** IS WHIZZING . . .

WHIZZ

HA-HA!

THIS WAY . . .

HA-HA!

WHIZZ

. . . AND THAT WAY

. . . HERE . . .

WHIZZ

HA-HA!

. . . AND THERE .

*YA

HA-HA!

WH

ER, WAKE UP, PIZAZZ

OK, NOW ALL WE HAVE TO DO IS SURROUND *THE WHIZZ* AND THEN SLOWLY MOVE IN, CLOSING IN ON HIM UNTIL HE HAS NOWHERE LEFT TO WHIZZ. NOW THIS PLAN ONLY WORKS IF WE ALL WORK AS A TEAM, OK...?

YAWN

R HEROES HAVE HIM SURROUNDED...

...OR DO THEY?

PIZAZZ!

ZZZZZ

HUH!

HA-HA!

OH, PIZAZZ!

EYE ROLL!

ZZZZZZZZZZZZZZZZZZZZZZZZZZZZZ

ERRR, PIZAZZ, AKE UP! WE NEED YOUR HELP...

WHAAAA? OH, YOU'LL BE FINE. IT'S JUST ANOTHER BADDIE, THERE'S ALWAYS ANOTHER.

SO OUR THREE AWAKE SUPERHEROES MAKE A PLAN...

MELTS HIMSELF AN IRON DOOR...

T'DAAA...

QUICK, DAD! *THE WHIZZ* IS COMING...

DAD SLAMS HIMSELF JUST IN TIME...

SLAM!

OWWW!

ALSO OWWW!!

...STOPPING THE WHIZZ IN HIS TRACKS!

YAY! THE WHIZZ IS CAUGHT, NO THANKS TO PIZAZZ. ER, PIZAZZ?

ZZZZZZ...

On the way home Mum kept going on and on about, 'WHERE HAD I **BEEN**?', 'WHY DIDN'T I **HELP** MORE?', 'WHY WAS MY T-SHIRT NOT TUCKED INTO MY SHORTS?' BLAH, BLAH, BLAH, Blah, blaaaaaaah...

Thanks, Mum, *charming*. But really, I couldn't do EVERYTHING. Or even ANYTHING this morning. Clearly. EYE ROLL

As soon as I got home I flopped on my bed. I mean, what else was there to do? RED suggested I read a book, but that would mean I'd have to HOLD it. Dad suggested I help cook lunch, but that would mean I'd have to ACTUALLY stand up. I think BERNARD invited me into her vocal harmony group, but that would mean vocally harmonising, and really I JUST

COULD NOT BE

BOTHERED.

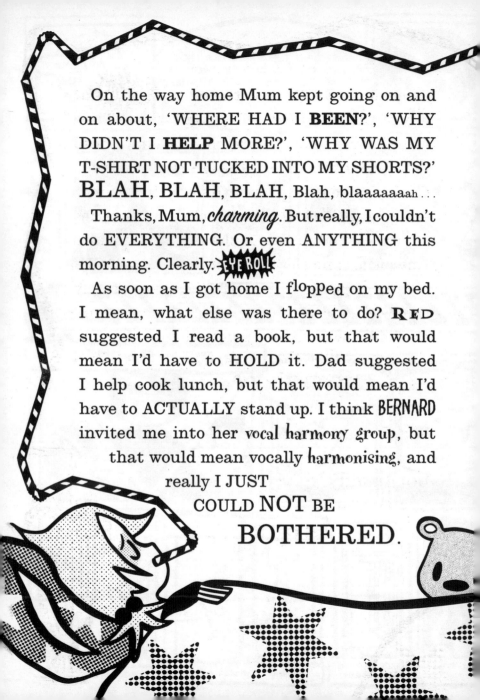

I couldn't EVEN be bothered to **EYE ROLL** at any of their RIDICULOUS suggestions. Then Mum brought me a sandwich. Er, thanks, but I really don't think I have the **energy** to eat it ... Couldn't she get me something a bit easier to eat, like a *milkshake* or some soup, with a series of straws? Or maybe cut the sandwich up into tiny pieces and slowly feed it to me? PLEASE?

Mum ***eyerolled*** – AHEM? – then left my sandwich and the room. I tried to say thank you, but it was just too much effort, so I didn't.

And then '**POW**' (but a really small, lacklustre POW) – **ANOTHER ME** was in the room.

I wondered which one it could be this time, but I only wondered for about one second, because, really, who could be bothered?

sigh . . .

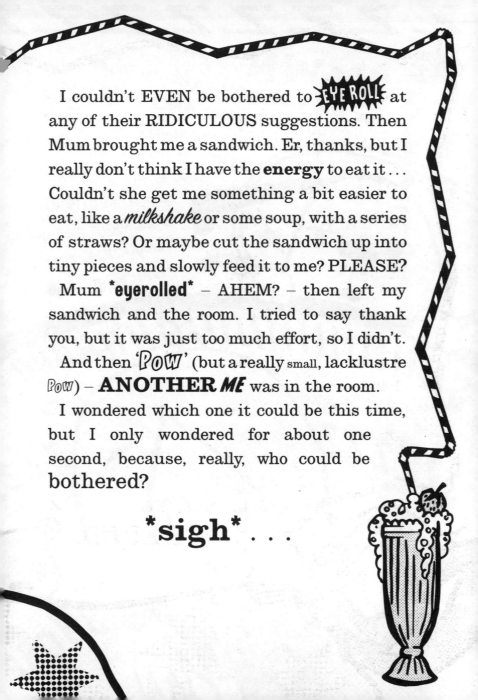

PIZAZZ'S TO-DO LIST

GET UP

CLEAR AWAY CRISP PACKETS ☑

DUST AWAY BISCUIT CRUMBS ☑

PUT ALL APPLE CORES IN BIN ☑

HANG UP CLOTHES (not on floor) ☑

ORGANISE NAIL POLISHES ☑

HANG UP ACCESSORIES ☑

SPRUCE UP TEDDY ☑

MAKE BED ☑

PUT JUICE CARTONS IN BIN ☑

PUT BOOKS ON BOOKSHELF ☑

MAKE BED

DO TO-DO LIST

AND THEN . . .

As I was jumping UP and DOWN on my freshly made bed with **RED**, super happy I had defeated my second-to-last *DEMON*, I felt

AMAZING

And then I realised that I was jumping UP and DOWN with my annoying little sister and suddenly felt **NOT quite so AMAZING** and **stopped** immediately. But I did thank her because I AM NOT A MONSTER!

Then we all went to **Grandma** and **Gramps's** house for dinner and I told **Gramps** all about my *DEMONS*, and while he was very *sympathetic* he also **laughed** SO MUCH he was almost constantly trumping little **fireballs** (a side effect of having **fire** as your *SUPER POWER* and being OLD), so **Grandma** made him stand outside with the fire extinguisher. But **Gramps** laughing makes ME **laugh too** (just WITHOUT the trumpy **fireballs**), and that made me feel a bit better about *THE DEMONS* and everything. After all, I only had one left to DEFEAT,

how HARD could it be?

EYE ROLL

The bit where things get AWKWARD . . .

I spent most of Sunday trying to work out WHO my LAST *DEMON* might be, when they might pop up and how I was ever going to defeat them. I talked to the BERNARDS about it and they were all full of suggestions – some were more *helpful* than others, and some were actually just PLAIN **RUDE** (I'm looking at YOU, STINK-EYE).

If anything, this just left me more confused than ever, so I called **Susie**, one of my best friends from my old school. *Brilliantly*, Tom was over at her house for tea, so we all discussed *THE DEMONS* and who on earth could be next. **Susie** was very *helpful* as she knows me better than nearly anyone, even my mum. She EVEN knows about the **LLAMA INCIDENT**.

Some of her suggestions were really quite, erm, honest, but then **Susie** always tells me the **TRUTH** and that is why she is such a **good** friend. Then Tom suggested some **FUNNY** ones, which is why he is such a **good** friend. Afterwards, we all talked about the next **ROLLER DISCO** and how **mushrooms** are **evil**, and then Tom's mum arrived at **Susie's** house to take him home so we all said goodbye and went.

THE NEXT DAY . . .

When I headed into school, I felt *slightly* prepared but mainly a bit worried as it would be just typical for my **BIG *DEMON* finale** to happen at school in front of everyone AND **Serena**. **RED** even gave me her special lump of **moon rock** for good luck and I was actually quite touched by this but managed to hide it almost *completely*.

I met **Ivy**, Molly and Ed at the main entrance to school and they all looked a bit *worried* too. I told them my TOP FIVE ideas about who my next evil ***DEMON*** would be. **Ivy** made another suggestion: ***HUFFY PIZAZZ***. Molly agreed and Ed even suggested ***CLUMZY PIZAZZ***. Er, thanks, guys. I wondered why I seemed to have the MOST honest friends in the **UNIVERSE**, but when they all promised to keep an eye out and said they would help me *however* they could, then I realised that **actually** I had the best friends in the **UNIVERSE**.

Even if they were EXTREMELY honest.

We were all at our desks when the bell went and **Mrs Harris** took the register, then she reminded me about the **HAPPINESS ASSEMBLY** later that day. Well, of course she didn't **actually** REMIND me about it because, of course, I hadn't **actually** *forgotten* it. NO, NOT AT ALL.

I wasn't going to let a *piffling* little thing like **FIVE *DEMON ME***'s distract me from a **HAPPINESS ASSEMBLY**.*

I rummaged around in my folder to try to find the piece of paper with my **ASSEMBLY** stuff on it, but then the **BELL** rang and we all had to go to class. I told myself it would be FIIIIIINE, but I don't think *I* believed **me**.

*I **was** and I absolutely **had** COMPLETELY FORGOTTEN.

The morning went so S…L…O…W…L…Y it was *agony*, and I knew I should use some of the extra SLOW time to read my **HAPPINESS ASSEMBLY** thing, but I JUST COULDN'T. I was on such **HIGH ALERT** that almost anything made me jᵘmp…

MY SHADOW…

A TREE…

At lunch I could *barely* eat (just some lasagne, peas, carrots, garlic bread, chocolate cake, a banana, an apple and a flapjack – I KNOW!) and all afternoon I had the FIDGETS.

It got to 2.15 p.m. and I slightly *relaxed* at the thought that my final DEMON was *probably* not going to be arriving today. THEN I remembered it was very nearly time for the HAPPINESS ASSEMBLY and I hadn't even read my bit once, let alone a few times, and then the BELL went and we all had to go to the big hall and it WAS TOO LATE. I grabbed the piece of paper Mrs Harris had given me last week and went along to the hall with everyone else, trying not to look too much like I was COMPLETELY panicking.

As soon as we arrived at the big hall Mrs Harris told me to go to the front with the other poor people who had also been made to read something out, *probably* against their will too. When I got there I tried to practise my bit, but my mind didn't seem to want to READ the words because it was too busy **panicking** and *imagining* all the AWFUL things that might be just about to happen . . .

OH NO

It is quite
believable that
I might start **LAUGHING**
UNCONTROLLABLY.

Or **CRYING!**

Or **BOTH!!**

UGH

What if
I start doing a
CHICKEN IMPRESSION
halfway through
my talk?

Well, that did it, I HICCUPPED. I hoped REALLY HARD that I had mistaken a worry burp for a HICCUP, and that it was just a one-off, but then it happened again . . .

NOOOOOOOOOO!

What next . . . ?

POOF!

Oh. *EMBARRASSED DEMON PIZAZZ.*

For my final battle.

In ASSEMBLY.

With the actual WHOLE SCHOOL watching.

That's what.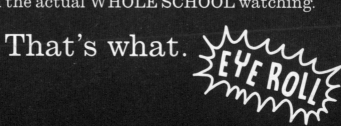

A really, really **SUPER** GOOD **SUPER POWER** would be disappearing. Or making the ground swallow you up when you are so **embarrassed** you are almost certain you are about to turn inside out from the COMPLETE *CRINGE* of it all. But all I had was jazz hands/glitter storm, and that was only ever going to make a situation **MORE** embarrassing rather than **less** embarrassing. Oh, and while I *can* fly, I was BANNED from doing it at school after I *accidentally* flew a goal in during netball.

What? It's a fine line between jumping really high and *actually* flying. Honest.

Super helpfully* ***EMBARRASSED DEMON PIZAZZ*** managed to think of a few **more** things that could go wrong when I did my reading and, while unlikely, just the thought of them made my **HICCUPS** get even faster . . .

NOOOOOO.

* Not helpfully

ONE BY ONE EVERYONE PICKED TO BE PART OF THE ASSEMBLY WALKS ON STAGE TO READ THEIR BIT OUT...

ALL OF A SUDDEN OUR HERO REALISES HICCUPS AREN'T SO BAD, IN FACT THEY ARE JUST, WELL, HICCUPS! MAYBE IF SHE THINKS ABOUT OTHER 'EMBARRASSING' THINGS THE SAME WAY, THEY WON'T BE EMBARRASSING EITHER. AND SO, IN FRONT OF THE **WHOLE SCHOOL** PIZAZZ DECIDES TO ...

AND SLOWLY BUT SURELY OUR HERO REALISES THAT **ALL** THE THINGS SHE THOUGHT WERE **EMBARRASSING** AREN'T REALLY THAT BAD AT ALL ... SO SHE DECIDES TO TUCK HER CAPE INTO HER PANTS, DANCE HER SOCKS OFF AND DO THE FUNKY CHICKEN (WITH SOUND EFFECTS) AMONG OTHER THINGS AND AS EACH EMBARRASSING THING IS MADE UNEMBARRASSING, EMBARRASSED DEMON PIZAZZ **SHRinks!!!!**

Well, I definitely NEVER imagined that doing **THE ROBOT** in front of the entire school would a) help me defeat a *BADDIE*, b) be SO MUCH FUN, and c) get me a **HUGE** round of **applause** – even *Serena* clapped! But not Andrew Wiggins as he never really seems to know what's going on and today was no exception, but I'm fine with that.

I guess when you figure out that the things you think are **embarrassing** are actually often *opportunities* to have a **LAUGH**, just slightly in disguise, then you realise that not that many things really ARE **embarrassing** after all.

10

The bit where I realise
the most important
thing of all . . .

Now my FIVE *DEMONS* were battled and I had won, I figured that was THAT! And now I had **nothing** to worry about EVER again. HA HA! Not really. I mean, I have my moments, but not even I am THAT much of a tw^{i}t.

I knew I still had my *DEMONS*, but now I knew it wasn't about having them or not having them . . . it was *actually* about knowing what to do with them when they popped up . . . I really, REALLY hoped they wouldn't pop up again in the form of whole actual other ME's, but you never know!

And I also knew that this time my friends had saved the day. Friends that had met my *DEMONS*, and STILL wanted to be my friends anyway! **Result!** I wondered how on earth I could ever thank them and figured that maybe doing the same thing for them and *their* *DEMONS* might be the way to go.

Then I shuddered because I was starting to worry myself with all the *sensible* thinking I was doing.

The End.

sigh Except it WASN'T!!

Just as I was starting to feel a smidge *relaxed* after, let's face it, a VERY trying week, then of course **CopyCat** *ZOOMED* into my actual school.

OH NO! What now? This was the **HAPPINESS ASSEMBLY** and she didn't belong here! She definitely didn't make me **HAPPY**, and possibly having to use my **SUPER POWER** in front of everyone was definitely something that made me TOTALLY UNHAPPY and I really didn't want **ANGRY/ANXIOUS/EMBARRASSED PIZAZZ** making another appearance.

Then I saw **Ivy**, Molly and Ed all **STARING** at me with a look that sort of said, 'YOU'VE got this . . . **PROBABLY** . . . But even if you HAVEN'T, we've got **YOU**,' and then they all raised their arms and did jazz hands, and then I realised that this was maybe the ULTIMATE TEST. If I could do this, if I could really BE **ME** (specifically the **me** with the REALLY embarrassing *SUPER POWER*) in front of THE WHOLE SCHOOL . . .

well, that would be a **good** thing . . .

right?

Right . . . ?

OUR HERO SPRINGS INTO ACTION, JAZZ HANDS/ GLITTER STORM IS GO! SHE CAPTURES BOTH THE MR EVANSES... JUST TO BE ON THE SAFE SIDE!

OH, PHEW! MUM AND AUNTY BLAZE ARRIVE TO TAKE OUR BADDIE AWAY.

BUT WHICH MR EVANS IS THE BADDIE?

WHA?

AFTER A FEW PROBING QUESTIONS AUNTY BLAZE WORKS OUT WHICH IS THE REAL MR EVANS AND WHICH ONE IS A SWELTERING, SLIGHTLY DAMP COPYCAT... AND TAKES HER/HIM AWAY TO MISSION CONTROL...

While I felt sorry for **CopyCat** being stuck as nylony Mr Evans, I also felt sort of happy for her that she had found her own thing, even if it did need a bit more work (if they weren't both **BADDIES**, I would have suggested she team up with **GIZMO KID**, but they are so I didn't). Who knew the **HAPPINESS ASSEMBLY** was for **SUPER BADDIES** too!

Mum said **Ivy**, Molly and Ed could come round for tea if they wanted as long as their parents said it was OK and they liked **CHILLI** (**Dad** was cooking, obvs). It turned out they did want to, their parents were fine about it and they all like **CHILLI** so . . .

When we got back home everyone went to my room but, as it doesn't seem to happen as often as I'd like, I hung back to tell **Mum** that *actually* she and **Aunty Blaze** had been WRONG about me having to defeat my ***DEMONS*** on my own. SURE, I had to do the actual battling, but without my friends (**UGH**, OK *and* my little **SISTER** who might have briefly NOT been annoying for about a split second) looking out for me, and being by my side, and knowing my ***DEMONS*** maybe even better than I did, I probably wouldn't have been able to defeat them at all. Well, I *might* have, but it would have taken A A A A A A G E S longer and probably have been quite a bit **messier**.

Mum smiled at me in a way that made me feel all weird, like she was *pleased* with me or like I had said something smart or like she was proud of me or something. **EYE ROLL** But then I **BURPED** 'Snacks, please!' and she looked at me like normal again. *Phew*.

The **Actual** End. But also . . .

. . . just THE BEGINNING . . .

Read all of Pizazz's *SUPER* adventures so far!